To Garrett,
Happy Recycling!
Nancy Van Laan
1995

ROUND AND ROUND AGAIN

Nancy Van Laan

Illustrated by Nadine Bernard Westcott

HYPERION BOOKS FOR CHILDREN
NEW YORK

FIRST EDITION
1   3   5   7   9   10   8   6   4   2

Library of Congress Cataloging-in-Publication Data

Van Laan, Nancy.
Round and round again / Nancy Van Laan;
illustrated by Nadine Bernard Westcott—1st ed.
p.   cm.
Summary: Mama recycles everything until the house is complete
with walls covered with candy wrappers and shingles that used to be
flapjack flappers, and the whole town turns out to see her handmade rocketship.
ISBN 0-7868-0009-7 (trade)—ISBN 0-7868-2005-5 (lib. bdg.)
[1. Recycling (Waste)—Fiction.   2. Stories in rhyme.]
I. Westcott, Nadine Bernard, ill.   II. Title.
PZ8.3.V47Ro   1994   813'.54—dc20
93-45918   CIP   AC

The artwork for each picture is prepared using gouache and pen and ink.
This book is set in 16-point Stone Informal.

For my daughter Jennifer, the environmentalist
–N.V.L.

For my niece Sarah
–N.B.W.

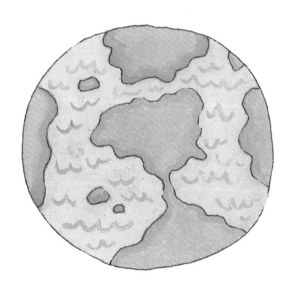

Let me tell you a story—it's funny but true—
how Mama changed old things into new.
She saved newspapers, plastic, tin.
Anything used, she used again.

She sang, "Round and round and round again,
over yonder and back again!"

Mama found a use for any old thing,
like a basketball net made of ribbons and string.

The rim of an old bike tire was the hoop
tacked on the back of our chicken coop.

Mama took old papers and tore them up.
She mixed some paste in a measuring cup.
She made us puppets, masks, and hats.
We put on a show for the dogs and cats!

They howled, "Round and round and round again,
over yonder and back again!"

Mama hated to see things thrown away.
This gave her a wild idea one day.

She hopped in her pickup. She drove up and down.
She filled it with goodies she found around town.

Over and over, she went back for more.
The things in our yard soon crept to the door.
When she returned with another load of stuff
we cried, "Oh, Mama! Enough is enough!"

But she kept singing, "Round and round and round again,
over yonder and back again!"

Mama got busy. She worked night and day.
She sorted through the junk like a hungry jay.

She measured all day. She pounded all night.
She told everybody, "You can help if you like."

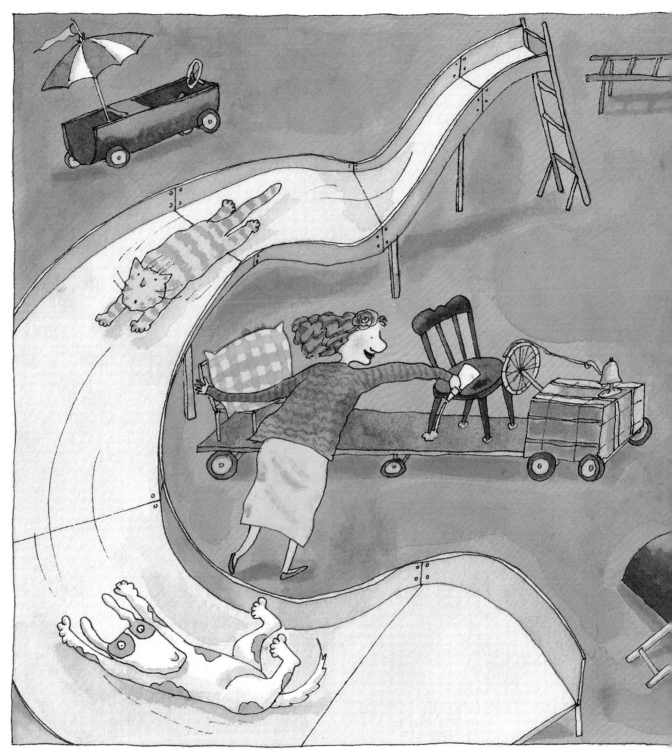

Soon we had slides! Seesaws, too!
And a go-cart made out of scraps and glue!
Swings were made out of fat truck tires.
They were hung with rope and telephone wires.

We swung round and round and round again,
over yonder and back again!

Now what was Mama trying to make?
It was round like the moon and rising like a cake.

We were itching to know. We started to fuss.
So Mama said, "It's a new house for us!"

She built the frame out of poles and crates,
barn sides, boat hulls, picket-fence gates.
She took a bunch of worn-out doors.
She laid them flat to make the floors.

We danced round and round and round again,
over yonder and back again!

The walls were covered with candy wrappers.
Shingles on the roof were flapjack flappers.

Ceiling tiles were baked like bread.
The porch was a great big bouncy bed!

Stairs were made out of old chair backs.
Window awnings were gunnysacks.
She used scrub boards to make the shutters.
Fruit-juice cans turned into gutters.

They wrapped round and round and round again,
over yonder and back again!

Mama said to use whatever we had,
so we painted the whole house rainbow plaid.

Old neon signs worked mighty fine
to light up the house like bright sunshine.

Some news reporters soon stopped by
to ask us how and what and why.
When they spread the word to give a hand,
the whole town came with a marching band!

They played round and round and round again,
over yonder and back again!

Smiling folks looked up, amazed.
Something high above them blazed.

It boomed. It zoomed. It spun in a dip.
It was us in a handmade rocketship!

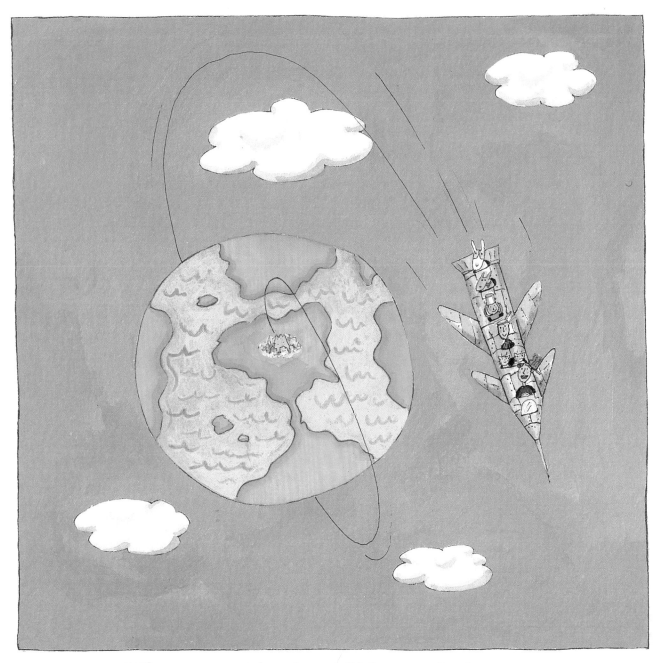

When we get back, we'll be so glad
to see what a good time everyone had
by using all the things they found
to make everything go round and round!

Now everybody sing, "Round and round and round again
over yonder and back again!"